Secrets
Hidden Below

THE ADAMSON ADVENTURES
1

The Adamson Adventures 1: Secrets Hidden Below
Second edition Copyright © Sandra Bennett 2021

ISBN: 978-0-6489382-1-7
Subjects: Children's fiction, Bali, treasure, adventure

Cover design by Nicola Matthews
Typesetting by Alycia M Tilley

Published by Rosella Ridge Books

SANDRA BENNETT
https://sandrabennettauthor.com/
First edition published by Elephant Tree Publishing

Australian National Library of Australia
Cataloguing in Publication Entry
Sandra D Bennett

Printed by Ingram Spark

To my three sons,

Thank you for providing the
inspiration and imagination that
enabled me to create this adventure.

Sandra Bennett, 2018

CHAPTER 1
Coconut Head

The heat is already unbearable. I'm hot, sweaty and clumps of damp sand have found their way into places they shouldn't. Even the sunscreen is melting.

'Hey, watch out dunderhead. Quit throwing sand in my face.'

'What's crawled up your back? A crab or something?' Luke threw a shovel of sand that landed in my lap. 'And don't call me a dunderhead, you're a kapala-kalapa.'

'Oh, very clever,' I clapped. 'If I'm a coconut head, then you're a kepala-pisang, a banana head.' I swiped at the flying sand as Luke tossed another shovel full at me. Then I reached to grab a handful to throw back at him. I was sick of sitting on this beach with him and Clare.

'Hey, cut it out you two.' Clare stopped digging her hole for a moment. 'You'll have sand in someone else's face in a minute, and then we will all be in trouble.'

'Don't be such a worry-wart.' Luke laughed and kicked a pile of sand back into Clare's ever-growing hole. 'Looks like you're digging your way to China'

'Might as well do something while Dad's out surfing and Mum's window shopping.' Clare sighed and began to dig again.

'Yeah but Dad did promise us an adventure on this holiday,' Luke smiled. 'There must be all sorts of possible adventures we could have here.'

'I know,' I agreed. 'Dad promised to take me snorkelling as well as surfing. So far it's been all about him and the waves.'

'Dad's reliving his youth. He says he was a bit of a legend surfer in his day.' Clare stopped digging for a moment and looked out towards the horizon in a search for Dad.

'Yeah, right. A legend in his own mind.'

It was day three of our holiday, and so far, we had spent all day every day here on Kuta beach while Dad surfed and Mum shopped for just the right souvenirs to take home to family and friends. Sure, he had taken me out for the occasional short surf with him, but I've mostly sat here with these two.

I was a bit annoyed. I need to be out there, where it's wet and cool. The water is so inviting. It's ideal surfing conditions. I've watched perfect waves roll in one after the other, for hours, but can I go out there and join Dad? No, I'm stuck here on the beach as usual with Clare and Luke. Why does Dad get to have all the fun? I thought this was supposed to be a family holiday. So far, it seems like Mum and Dad get to do what they want, while I babysit my brother and sister.

'I read this great article the other day when I googled the best spots to snorkel in Bali. Dad promised we would go there. It's only a couple of hours up the coast.'

'Geez Zac, a couple of hours in the car in this heat? I don't think so.' Luke shook his head.

'The car's got aircon you dufus. Besides, you'd like it. The reef is made from the remains of a sunken WW2 wreck and has lots of Nemo fish swimming around it too.'

'Well, that makes it all worthwhile then,' Luke grinned. 'But stop calling me names you kepala-kelapa.' He threw a handful of sand at me again. This time I was ready for it and ducked.

'So, original Luke.'

The sand flew over my shoulder and landed on the back of a guy who was in the middle of an oil massage.

'Watch it, kid,' he jumped and shouted.

'Oops, sorry mate,' I replied and turned to give Luke a nasty glare. The sticky heat and stench of incense mixed with tanning lotions and salty air was getting to all three of us. Clare stopped to wipe the back of her arm across her forehead before she flung sand further into the air with her plastic shovel.

'Crikey! I hit something!' She sounded stunned.

CHAPTER 2
A Secret Hidden Below the Sand

'What?' I grumbled and swatted a fly. 'It's something really hard, and it makes a clunk when I hit it with my shovel.' She dug with more frantic energy. It wasn't likely she would find anything of interest buried at this beach, probably just a bit of junk. If Dad wasn't about to take me on that snorkelling trip, I might as well sort the shells I had gathered. So far, I had found quite a few colourful and unusual shaped ones on our walks along the beach trying to keep these two occupied. My new shell collection was of a lot more interest to me than anything Clare might find down a stupid hole.

Sand began to fly in all directions. Clare never worked that hard at anything in her life, especially in this heat. Maybe there was something of interest down there after all.

'Hey, slow down and let me see.' I tried to push her out of the way so that I could see into her cavernous hole. She refused to let me get a look and pushed me back out of the way. We began to wrestle in the sand. Our arms and legs thrashed as we tried to push each other out of the way until I felt Luke tug at me until he pulled us apart.

'What are you guys fighting for? It's just a hole.' Luke had managed to push both of us out of the way so he could peer down into the hole himself. He reached down to dust off the remains of the sand. 'Wow! Look what I've found!' Luke began to dust off an old green bottle. It was much bigger than anything I had expected.

'Give that back! It's mine!' Clare tried to yank the bottle from Luke's grasp.

'Finders keepers.' Luke turned away from us and held it up towards the sun to look inside. 'Cool! There's a secret message in this thing.'

Clare reached out again. This time she succeeded. She yanked the bottle from Luke's hands, 'It's mine. I found it, so I'll be the one to see what's in it!'

She ran away from us as fast as she could. The chase was on. The three of us raced along the beach. We darted in and out between sunbaking holidaymakers, food carts and a mass of beachwear sellers. Hawkers and tourists all yelled at us to watch where we were going. With one final tackle Clare, Luke, and I all crashed to the ground, spitting out the taste of Bali sand.

'Okay, okay!' I took a few deep breaths. 'Let's all have a look.'

Clare pulled out the cork and tipped the bottle upside down. The paper inside slid into Luke's outstretched hands. Careful not to tear the worn paper he unrolled it gently. We gazed at the paper, it was faded, brown and burnt around the edges.

'It's a map!'

Clare and I leaned closer over Luke's shoulder and stared in amazement.

'Do you think it could be a treasure map?'

Luke clutched it tightly. 'Maybe some pirates stole a huge treasure from some rich king. Maybe they buried the treasure somewhere here on this tropical island because they thought it was uninhabited. Then, before they could return to collect it, they were chased by a Spanish Armada, and a big battle took place.'

Luke stood up and pretended to wield a sword. As he continued his story. 'Guns and cannons were firing in all directions, there was a sword fight to the death. But the pirate captain kept a secret map and threw it overboard in this bottle, just in time, before he was captured or worse, killed.' He flung himself to the ground in an over exaggerated death scene.

'No, don't be stupid.' I shook my head. 'You're letting your imagination run wild as usual.'

'But what if it is!' Luke's eyes popped. He gulped in a deep breath.

'Do you think we should try to find out?' Clare bit at a fingernail.

'Let's go on a treasure hunt!' Luke grinned.

'I knew you were going to say that. Will there be a treasure chest? Will it be dangerous?' Clare shuffled her feet in the sand. While Luke had a wild imagination, Clare would never take a risk in anything. They were chalk and cheese.

'Just imagine if there really was a treasure chest and it was filled with gold and jewels. We could be rich!' Luke grabbed Clare by the shoulders. 'Think of all the things we could buy. A new Play Station, upgrade our computer, a motor-bike and robots. We could have anything we want!'

'I could have my own science lab in the backyard, with heaps of chemicals, a microscope and plenty of room for my shell and rock collections.' The idea of a treasure hunt sounded not so bad after all. It would give us something better to do than sit on the beach all day.

'What about the cubby house I always wanted to build. With ropes, ladders, slides, castle turrets, the lot,' Luke continued. 'And not to forget a bike track. Or even our own pirate ship to sail the seven seas and go on fantastic adventures.' Luke really was getting carried away now.

'Shhh! Not so loud.' I had a feeling that someone was listening to us. I felt the hairs on the back of my neck prickle. The beach had become crowded in the heat of the late afternoon sun. This is Kuta Beach, one of the most popular tourist destinations in all of Bali. I could see and hear hawkers everywhere.

'Want a massage?'

"You have manicure? Yes?'

'See my batik, very beautiful. You buy?'

Some people tried to barter for the best bargain. Others seemed to just accept the price. I guess you can tell the tourists that had been here before, they seemed to know the routine.

Other people shooed the hawkers away. They wanted to be left in peace to enjoy the sun.

I looked at the girl having her hair beaded, she had her eyes closed. Probably half asleep, or daydreaming. A group of teenage girls were having their fingers and toenails painted. Boy, they made enough noise with their talk and laughter. They didn't seem to be paying any attention to three Aussie kids fighting on the sand. What about that guy not far from us that we threw sand on earlier, in the middle of his oil massage? He looked really relaxed, bet he could have heard everything we said. I shrugged, who would believe it anyway? A secret message in a bottle hidden deep below in the sand. What were the chances? Probably some kind of joke.

'I'm going on a treasure hunt!' Luke broke my concentration as he jumped to his feet and placed his hands on his hips. 'Are you two with me or not?'

'Quiet!' I held a finger to my lips, but I could tell he wasn't listening to me as usual.

'We all agreed we wanted an adventure. Here's our chance and maybe find a secret treasure too. I'm going, even if I have to do it alone.' Luke stretched and began to walk back up the beach.

I jumped to my feet to join Clare. While

she brushed the sand off her legs, I wiped the sweat from my face and glared at the back of my annoying little brother, Luke.

'Who knows what sort of trouble he is about to get us into now? But I guess we better go with him.'

'Oh dear, I have a feeling this could be dangerous.' Clare bit her lip and shuffled off towards Luke.

CHAPTER 3

Driftwood

I brushed the sand off my arms and legs and searched the horizon for Dad. Was he ever going to come out of the surf? Well, there wasn't much point hanging around here. I grabbed my towel. Best to go after Luke, who knew what his numbskull brain was plotting now.

I couldn't help but take one last look around. The hairs on the back of my neck still stood on end. I could hear an annoying click, over and over. 'What was that?'

It was the guy from the oil massage. He now sat forward and flipped open and closed the lid of a gold lighter.

His eyes pierced into mine. A strange, uneasy feeling washed over me.

I stole a second glance. He looked down for a moment. The sun hit the gold of his lighter, and it reflected straight into my eyes. I had to put my hand up to shield them as he continued to flick and play with it. I felt a shiver run down my spine.

He raised his eyes to mine again. A sly, crooked yellow grin slowly emerged. I tried to turn away, then I saw it. The tattoo! Beads of sweat dripped from his upper arms, the tattoo on his left arm glistened in the sun. It was a picture of a huge, ugly red-back spider. Talk about creepy. I'd recognise those nasty little things anywhere, they're all through our garden back home. Why would anyone want a tattoo like that? I shivered again and forced myself to turn away and tried one last time to search for Dad.

I still couldn't see Dad anywhere, but Mum strode straight towards me. Amazed that Luke had left the map behind, I grabbed it, pushed it back into the bottle and hid it under the back of my T-shirt before she could see. The creepy feeling that someone is watching me, came back. The stranger's eyes felt like they burnt a hole through the back of my shirt.

'What are you up to Zac?' Mum stood before me, her arms crossed, shopping bags hung from each arm. Her eyes glared at me. 'I know you're hiding something, what is it?'

'Um, nothing,' I crossed my fingers behind my back and wished she hadn't noticed.

'Where have your brother and sister disappeared to? You were supposed to be looking after them.'

'Hey, here comes Dad,' I tried to change the subject and began to race towards him. I left Mum and the stranger behind. Did those eyes still follow me? I couldn't make myself look back over my shoulder. I didn't really want to know.

As Dad left the waves, I watched him tuck his surfboard under one arm. He held something else under the other.

'What have you found there, Dad?'

He put his arm around my shoulders and handed it to me.

'It's a bit of driftwood for you.' He winked and patted me on the back. 'I found it onshore just a bit further north of here. Thought you might be interested. Maybe it's off the wreck you wanted to go see. Should we go check it out tomorrow?' Without waiting for my answer, he jogged off. He spotted Mum who had caught up to Luke and Clare and raced to catch up to them. Then, with a sideways grin at Luke, he called out over his shoulder. 'Perhaps it's off an old sunken pirate ship!'

I stood still and looked at the piece of driftwood I now found in my hands. Funny Dad found this the same day we found the treasure map. As I turned it over, I saw the remains of some ancient markings. Something seemed to be painted on it. I couldn't quite make out what it said. Perhaps there was some hint of truth to Luke's wild story after all. I blinked and washed the salt from my eyes as I tried to take a better look. Between the glare from the sun that reflected on the water and the scratched, worn old bits of paint it was near impossible to read. I shook my head, now who was letting his imagination get the better of him?

CHAPTER 4
Whispers in the Night

Over a huge bowl of nasi goreng, Indonesian fried rice, back in our hotel room that evening Clare, Luke and I began to study the mysterious markings painted on the driftwood. It had me intrigued. This was a bit like being a real archaeologist making some strange find, but not yet knowing if the discovery had any real significance.

'Do you think it's from a real pirate ship?' Luke asked. 'I bet it's from the same one the pirate threw the bottle overboard from.'

'Hold your horses, Luke. Just slow down a minute.' I shoved him out of the way. 'We don't have any evidence yet. Don't you know scientists research their discoveries before they reach a conclusion.'

'Zac,' said Luke as he pushed back in front

of me. 'Did you bring your mini science kit?'

'Of course. You know I don't go anywhere without it. Especially when Dad said he would take me snorkelling on a reef. You never know what I might have found to clean and examine.'

It didn't take long to realise exactly what he was after. I rummaged around in my bag for a moment then pulled out the kit. Inside was a paintbrush perfect for wiping away dust and sand.

I was beginning to be curious about this piece of driftwood.

'Don't you think it was strange that Dad happened to find this on the same day we had uncovered a secret treasure map in a bottle that had been buried in the sand for who knows how long?'

'Bit of a coincidence.' Clare nodded.

'Maybe someone's been snooping around a pirate shipwreck, and it came loose.' Luke's eyes were wide with excitement.

'Here we go with your crazy ideas again.'

I shook my head and began to wipe away some of the sand in the crevices. 'Besides, someone snorkelling around a wreck doesn't explain the message hidden in the sand.'

'Maybe they were hoping to find a clue in the shipwreck?' Luke wasn't about to drop his theory. 'Maybe they were searching for the map but didn't know the pirate had thrown it overboard.'

'This is getting ridiculous. Let's just examine the evidence before we jump to any more conclusions.' I tried to concentrate on the driftwood instead of Luke's silly ideas.

With each careful stroke, we brushed away all the years of salt and sand that had collected in all the tiny crevices. The paint of each letter was badly eroded from exposure with the constant battering of waves and searing heat of the tropical sun.

'It's no use.' Clare slumped back in her chair. 'We'll never be able to work this out.'

'Probably is pure coincidence anyway,' I tried to reassure her. 'First a message in a bottle, then a clue on a piece of driftwood. It does sound far-fetched. No one would believe us if we told them.'

Then I paused and scratched my head, my mind flashed back to the stranger at Kuta Beach. He had seemed very interested in what we found. I shivered as that same uneasy feeling came over me again. Now I was letting my imagination get the better of me, just like Luke. Should I tell the others? No, no need to alarm them without any proof. A scientist doesn't jump to conclusions, and here I was assuming something creepy, perhaps dangerous, about some guy on the beach without any evidence. I decided to try and forget the strange man if I could.

'Room service,' called a voice from the corridor as a knock tapped the door. Quickly we hid the map and driftwood before I opened the door to let in a waiter.

'There must be a mistake,' I said. 'We didn't order anything.'

'Oh sorry, my apologies for disturbing you.' The waiter looked around our room before he went to leave.

'Hang on,' Luke stopped him. 'You're not Indonesian what are you doing working here?'

'Don't be so nosey' I scolded him. 'It's none of our business.'

The waiter smiled.

'That's OK,' he assured us. 'I'm on a working holiday from Holland.'

'Been here long?' Luke continued to ask.

'No, not long.' The waiter shrugged. 'Now I really must see who this food belongs to.' He left after one last look around the room.

'That was a bit strange.' Clare had a worried frown again.

'Everyone makes mistakes Clare.' Luke shrugged.

I agreed and went back to help Luke who continued to painstakingly work away on the driftwood. Now he had a black marker pen and began to attempt to fill in the gaps. One by one, like the bits and pieces of a jigsaw puzzle the words started to take shape before our eyes.

BATAVIA – DUTCH EAST INDIES.

'Yes! I knew it!' Luke jumped up and punched the air. 'This is off an old pirate ship.'

'Sorry to dampen your enthusiasm,' I said as I took a closer look. 'It's more than likely just off an old trading ship that ran aground in a storm. Jakarta was a major shipping port for years. It was known as Batavia and was a Dutch colony.'

'I know all that Zac. I do listen at school.' Luke smiled. He considered that remark for a moment. 'Sometimes. But this proves it comes from the same time as the map. It has to be off a pirate ship!'

'Hang on, we don't know how old the map is, or even if it's real!' said Clare.

'Then why don't we have a good look at the map and see what we can find out?' The colour rose in Luke's cheeks. He stood with his hands on his hips and looked around the room. 'Where did you hide the bottle anyway Zac?'

Just then, Dad appeared at our bedroom door. He leaned against the frame and smiled. 'Lights out boys and girls. Have you got your torches? Beware of ghosts and things that go bump in the night.' He had a little chuckle and closed the door. We all knew who Luke got his imagination from. Dad was always quick with a joke. The door opened just enough for one last laugh. 'Goodnight, don't let the bedbugs bite.'

Left to ourselves, I slid the bottle out from under my pillow. Torches in our hands, we dove beneath my covers. Once again, I removed the cork and slipped out the treasure map.

'Well, what can you see? What does it say?'

'Don't be so impatient,' I said to Luke as I squinted trying to get a better look. 'Don't we have a magnifying glass around here somewhere?' Luke rummaged through my science kit, then began to search the beds and our suitcases, that were still flung in the corner of the room in our hurry a couple of days ago to unpack and get to the beach.

'I've got it!' he exclaimed.

'Quiet, you'll wake Mum and Dad,' I whispered with slight annoyance.

'Sorry, Zac. Give me a look!' As Luke

grabbed the map, he ripped the corner that had been in my hand.

'I don't believe it!' Luke pointed in surprise. 'There's actually an X that marks the spot on here!'

'Where? What spot?' I doubted it but leaned in even closer to see, just in case he was right.

'Right there!' He pointed to a piece of coastline just a bit further northeast of here. There was a funny looking picture of a temple in the sea with a half sun setting in its shadow.

'Quick, someone find our maps of Bali!' I waved a hand around our room. 'Is there anything like it on one of them? How far up the coast is it?'

We looked at one and then the other. Then Luke found it on a map.

'There it is. It's a temple, and it's called Tanah Lot.' He began to read the information out loud. 'Come and see our mystical temple. Catch a photograph of the beautiful silhouette at sunset. See the mysterious caves and their guardian snake.' Luke put the map in his lap and stared at Clare and me.

'Snakes. No way. I don't like the sound of snakes.' Clare shook her head and bit another nail.

'That's it!' Luke ignored Clare and pointed to the temple on the map. 'That's where we have to go tomorrow!'

CHAPTER 5

Tanah Lot Temple

'Surf's up!' Dad walked into our room and rubbed his hands together excitedly. I managed to open one eye to see the sun had begun to creep over the horizon. It was far too early for any normal or sane person to be out of bed, only my Dad and other crazy surfer dudes get up at dawn.

'Here we go again, another day at the beach.' I groaned and rolled over to try to ignore him, then I remembered.

'What happened to doing what I wanted to do today?'

'I know I promised to take you snorkelling around that reef, but the surf's up dude.' Dad smiled.

'Dad, I've got a better idea.'

'What could be better than an early morning surf? Isn't that what we came to Bali to do? Surf, sun and sand, can't think of anything better.' Dad raised one eyebrow and rubbed the stubble on his chin with his fingers.

'How about we all explore some caves?' I tried not to sound too enthusiastic as I couldn't have him believe I'm into doing too much with the family. It didn't sound too far-fetched, it was rock related, and he knew I was crazy about that.

'So, you'd rather go explore some caves now, instead of that reef you've been nagging about for days?' Dad raised an eyebrow. 'Which caves did you have in mind, Zac?'

'Last night we had a look at our map of Bali.' I picked it up to show him. 'There are a few caves not that far from here, and I'm sure Mum would love to see the temple.' I knew this would help sway my argument. Dad grinned, then nodded.

'Sounds good to me Zac,' he tapped me on the shoulder. 'But I'm still having that surf.

Anyone care to join me? I can smell that fresh sea air and hear the waves calling.'

'No Dad,' Clare barely opened her eyes. 'That's the smell of incense, it's everywhere over here.'

'Sure Dad.' Luke sprang to his feet and pulled on his swimmers, he smiled from ear to ear. I guess he thought the same as me, keep Dad happy, and before long we would be on our way. Clare groaned, rolled over and covered her head with her pillow.

As soon as Dad and Luke left I jumped back onto my bed. I laid my head on the pillow with my hands resting underneath and looked up at the ceiling. This was going to be an even greater holiday than any of us had ever imagined.

I must have dozed back off to sleep because the next thing I heard Mum call out.

'Zac, for the last time, get up. We're leaving in two shakes of a lamb's tail!' I knew I'd better move, I only had a few minutes.

As I grabbed my backpack, I threw in our

torches, all the bits of my mini science kit, my swimmers and a hat, and the most essential thing of all, the treasure map.

The three of us sat crammed in the back of the hire car without a spoken word between us. I watched lush green tiered fields of rice paddies race past, one after the other. The coast road seemed to meander forever. I began to give up any hope of ever getting there when finally, Dad turned into a car park.

Clare, Luke and I were off and running.

'Hey, slow down,' I heard Mum call. 'What's the hurry?'

'Just trying to avoid the rush of all the tourists,' I shouted back as I turned around and jogged backwards to see if Mum and Dad were going to try to catch up to us. I saw Mum shrug her shoulders and laugh. She slipped her hand into Dad's as they wandered down the path. They paused here and there to look in makeshift shops full of sarongs and batiks. I pulled my hat out of my bag and put it on. Mum and Dad would be ages yet. We had plenty of time to explore.

Before long we found ourselves on a flat stone platform, and a few local Balinese people sat with their feet dangled over the edge. To my surprise, I could hear them speaking, and I managed to understand the odd word or two. Their local dialect was not quite the same as the Bahasa Indonesia I was learning at school, but there were enough similarities for me to at least attempt to say hello.

'Selamat pagi. Apa Kabar?' I nodded to the group.

'Baik-baik saja dan kamu?' One replied with a smile and waved to us to sit.

'We are very well, thank you.' I said as we joined them.

They were kind enough to switch to English when they heard we were Australian. We chatted for a while, and they told us about the cracked old stairs we had just come down. The stairs were so ancient they had worn away over hundreds of years from all the people that had walked the path to the temple, keen to pay homage to the guardian spirits of the sea.

'Balinese are big believers in spirits and

ghosts.' I whispered to Luke and Clare.

'We know.' Luke gave me a little shove. 'We're not stupid.'

'Yeah, I remember our Indonesian teacher said something about their type of Hindu religion being animist. They are very superstitious.' Clare nodded.

I looked ahead of us to more rocky steps that continued all the way down to the sand and eventually wound around the point towards Tanah Lot. There was another pathway lined with thick overhanging trees and more steps that climbed to the cliff top. I could see more stalls too, full of food and drinks, and sarongs, and t-shirts, and woodcarvings. Plenty to keep Mum and Dad busy for hours.

'Well, which way do you think?' said Luke as I watched his eyes follow the direction of both paths.

'Let's try going up to the top of the platform,' I pointed. 'We can take another look at the map when we get up there. Maybe we'll be able to figure out where to begin to look from there.' I really had no idea, but we had come this far, it was worth a try.

Clare gasped for breath as we all panted from our run up the steps in the heat.

'Wow!' she said. 'You've got to admit it sure does look pretty spectacular from here.'

There the temple stood for all to see. There was a combination of man-made structures among the cave and rock systems. Rugged stone arches carved one upon the other, dark caves formed within. Trees were jutting out in all directions providing a canopy sheltering the people who worshipped inside. At the very top, the Balinese people had constructed an open-air temple with a roof that appeared to me to look like split open coconut shells. One section was in layers, and it held its head high above the rest. I could see that the whole temple and rock formation was surrounded by the sea.

'Earth to Zac!' Luke waved a hand in front of my face. 'Don't worry about the view.'

'Sorry, I just needed a minute to look at the rocks.'

'We've got more important things to think of.' Luke had the treasure map out to try to work out where to go from here. 'I think our best bet,' he pointed, 'is to start in the caves directly under here.'

'Oh dear' Clare bit her bottom lip. 'I knew you were going to say that! You have to start somewhere dark and damp.' Even before Clare had finished her sentence, Luke had sprung to his feet. 'He's already forgotten about the snakes.'

He had taken off at lightning speed.

'Wait for us!' I called as we scrambled to catch up.

CHAPTER 6

Something in the Shadows

Luke paddled through soggy sand and slid over stones.

'Be careful!' he called back to us. 'These rocks are really wet and slippery.'

'What's the problem?' I asked as we almost reached him. Luke had come to an abrupt stop. He looked from side to side.

'There's a water channel here. It must be high tide. I can't find a narrow enough spot to get across.'

'So, what?' Luke and I were both surprised by Clare's response. She was always the cautious one, always concerned about what Mum would think. We all knew Mum's thoughts on the subject of wet, smelly shoes.

'Come on, let's go then.' Luke shrugged

as he splashed straight through the middle. 'Hurry up, before Mum and Dad get a chance to catch up.'

Clare and I didn't need any further encouragement. We were right behind him. We all raced towards the point.

'Wow. Look at the size of those cliffs,' said Clare.

I raised a hand to the peak of my hat and shifted it a little higher. The cliffs must have been made from the volcanic shoal. The erosion from the force of the waves and the monsoonal rains and winds crashing against them over thousands of years had caused many large cracks and crevices. Jagged rocks and fallen logs lay everywhere.

'There must be hundreds of caves around here.' Luke didn't seem to know which way to turn, or which cave to head to first. He darted from one opening to the next.

'Slow down Luke. You're running around like a chook with its head chopped off. You'll never find anything running around madly like that. If there is a treasure buried somewhere around here, it's not going to be easy to find. We need to make a plan.' I suggested Luke and Clare look in one direction while I explored the caves in the opposite. 'Let's look in each cave in order, not in random chaos.'

'So, what are we actually looking for?' Clare asked as she came out of the entrance of a narrow cave.

'I don't know exactly.' Luke shook his head. 'Maybe a cave with a secret entrance further inside or something.'

'Here we go with your wild imagination again. First, it's pirates, now it's secret entrances.' I ran my hand across a ledge just in case anyway. Just then I felt the hairs on my back stand on edge again. I froze as an eerie dark shadow flickered over me. I spun around. There it was, that same annoying sound, the continuous click of a lighter. No, it couldn't be. Was there someone lurking in the shadows? Was someone following us? A smell of massage oil wafted over me. I turned only to catch a quick glimpse of a man sliding into the shadows of a nearby rock face. He seemed vaguely familiar, but I only had a quick glimpse. It could have been anyone. Was that a tattoo I had seen on his arm? With caution, I stepped towards where I had seen him last, but he had gone.

I looked down, there were scuffed footprints left behind in the damp sand.

I took off my hat to wipe my forehead and scanned the area. As I did, I thought I caught a glimpse of a man's shadow slipping into the caves beneath Tanah Lot. It had to be the same man, there was no one else down here. It was dark in there, I didn't see him for long. I had just decided to follow him when I heard Luke shout with excitement.

'I think I've found it!'

Clare and I raced to where Luke was pointing. Sure enough, deep within the crevices of the cliff was a low-lying cave. I gazed at the steps that had been carved out of the stone. It was obvious many feet had trodden here before us. We were definitely not the only people who had come to explore this cave.

As I entered, I stopped to allow my eyes

to adjust to the sudden lack of light. It was so bright and hot outside, in contrast in here was so dark it took a while for my eyes to adjust. The air felt thick with the smell of incense and perspiration.

To my surprise I saw an old Balinese man sitting on a ledge, he beckoned us to join him. His face was wrinkled and weathered with the age of someone who has spent a lifetime in the sun. He did have a big broad smile, although that revealed his stained and broken teeth. He must have been a smoker for years.

'Selamat datang, welcome. Duduk, sit. Come join me where it is cool.'

He seemed harmless enough, even friendly as he welcomed us and gestured for us to sit down beside him.

'I show you something.' He smiled an even broader smile and pointed to another ledge above our heads. I couldn't quite see, but I knew something was there and it was alive!

CHAPTER 7

The Snake Legend

Clare and Luke's eyes were fixed above them. Their mouths were open wide. I heard a hiss come from above. Then a forked tongue appeared, followed by the head of a thick brown snake as it slithered to the edge of the ledge. In the faint light, we could see the underside of the snake's head and just make out its body coiled across the ledge. The three of us jumped and banged our heads on the roof of the cave as we rushed to back away.

'Look at the size of that thing! It's huge!' Clare took another step back to stand behind me.

'He will not bite,' the old man laughed and waved at us to come closer. He pointed again and shone a small torch in the direction of the snake's body.

'Come, you can touch him, but stay away from his head.' He nodded as he tried to reassure us, but I don't think any of us were convinced. Clare shook her head and took a few small steps backwards.

Should have known Luke would be the one to shuffle forward. Almost, as if in slow motion, he reached upwards with his right hand. I watched his hand quiver as it hovered over the top of the snake's body. I held my breath. Luke bit his bottom lip and lightly pressed his fingertips to the snake's skin.

'Talk about creepy, it feels so cold,' he said as he ran his fingers along the snakes back.

'Come on Zac. You should feel this.' Luke grinned and stepped back to make room for me.

'No thanks,' I shook my head. 'Think I'll pass on this one.'

The old man patted his hand on the rock ledge for us to sit beside him again.

'You want to hear story?' he asked. 'I tell you story of this cave, this sacred snake, yes?'

'Yes,' nodded Luke. We sat beside him,

Clare stayed by the cave entrance. She didn't take her eyes off the snake.

'Baik, good,' he smiled. Huddled next to Luke, we listened as he began to tell his story. All the while I kept one eye on the snake not so far above us.

'Ancient legend says this snake cave here for reason. Good reason.' He paused for a moment and leant closer to us. 'Many believe the snake here to protect temple. He part of this sacred place.' He pointed out towards Tanah Lot. 'People say snake leave cave at night, go to temple to guard against evil spirits or anybody who go there. When sun come up, he come back to cave for rest. But some people say snake cave here to protect another secret.'

I ran my fingers through my hair to brush it off my face. Now we were getting somewhere. This story was about to get interesting. The old man looked around the cave and lowered his voice to a whisper as he continued.

'Some say many years ago, long before my grandfather's grandfather, a tall ship with big white sails came to this beach. It stayed many hours. Two white men come ashore. They carry something very heavy. They disappear all night. One more man followed later. When sun come up, only one white man come back. He carry nothing. Legend say they come to this cave and bury treasure. Big tall ship, she begin to sail away. Not get very far. Big Boom! Ship on fire, it sink.' He shook his head. 'Nobody swim to shore. Other two white men never come out of caves. Nobody ever find treasure. Snake,' he said as he pointed above us. 'Snake knows secret hiding place of treasure.'

The old man stared silently at us and began smiling once more.

'I think I go walk now. Stretch my weary old legs,' he laughed as he stood ready to leave us. With a wink, he waved and was gone.

Clare's face was white. I'm not sure if it was with fear or excitement.

I looked at Luke as he scratched away at the wall surface, then back at Clare. She still stood at the cave's entrance.

'So, do we believe the old man's story?' I asked.

'Balinese do tend to believe in strange spirits.' Clare agreed. 'Doesn't make any of this real.'

'Come on guys. This is it.' Luke whispered. 'This has got to be the place. We've got the map, the driftwood and now we have the old man's story. What else do we need? The treasure must be around here somewhere.' His voice was becoming louder. Luke scrambled to his feet and began to search the cave.

'Aren't you forgetting something?' Clare asked him.

'No, what?' Luke stood with his hands on his hips.

Clare and I looked at each other, then Luke. Then together we said, 'THE SNAKE!'

CHAPTER 8
Ruby Eyes

'Somehow we have to coax that snake down off that ledge,' Luke stood with his hands on his hips and stared at the snake.

'Well, it's not going to be me. I'm not going anywhere near it, I'm arachnophobic.' Clare stamped her feet together and firmly crossed her arms.

'Arachnophobic means you're scared of spiders stupid, not snakes,' I shook my head and laughed a little. She didn't need to know I was feeling a bit nervous too.

'OK, well them too! I'm still not going anywhere near it!' Clare nodded towards the snake and kept her hands firmly folded. She shuffled a few more steps back, any more steps and she would be well out of the cave.

'I bet there's a secret passage hidden behind it.' Luke began to run his hands along the wall of the cave. 'Help me look for a hole or hidden gap, anything that might help us move away some of this rock.' He turned and pleaded with me. 'There has to be a tunnel here somewhere!'

I looked at my brother and sister, one was frantically scraping rock from the wall with his bare fingers, while the other refused to move. Neither wanted to face the snake, and I guess I didn't really either.

'Are you going to help or just stand there all day?' Clare was beginning to annoy me.

'I didn't want to come here in the first place, remember?' She shook her head and still refused to move.

'We all agreed on this adventure. You need to help,' I said.

'I didn't agree to anything dangerous, and I'm not going anywhere near that snake.' Clare folded her arms and refused to budge.

I shrugged my shoulders and joined Luke.

It wasn't worth arguing any further. Who cares if Clare misses out. We had to try something. I followed Luke's lead and thumped the stone walls with my fists. Over and over our hands scrambled, scratched and pushed, but always careful not to go too close to the snake.

'I give up!' I slumped against a large heavy rock and rubbed my sore hands together.

'Did you see that?' Luke grabbed my arm as the ledge slid out a bit wider. 'Wow! How did that happen?'

'It happened at the same time as I lent on this rock.' I turned, and with all my strength, gave the rock another push. The ledge moved again, and in one quick motion, the snake fell, it landed on the ground at our feet. It reared up in annoyance, hissed and spat. Clare jumped, Luke screamed, as he tried to push past me and raced for the front of the cave.

'That scared the living daylights out of me!' Clare shivered even though the temperature outside in the heat of the sun was near boiling.

My heart pounded deep within my chest

as we turned to look at the snake from a safer distance.

'Wow! Would you look at the size of that thing! It's huge!' said Luke. 'Do you think it's poisonous?'

I stretched my arms out in front of Luke and Clare as we very slowly edged a few steps forward.

'Well, the snake's off the ledge, Luke!' Clare whispered. We stood there in silence, our eyes glared at the snake, it glared back at us.

'WWWhat's that between his eyes?' Luke pointed.

'Looks like a jewel.' I whispered back. 'In fact, I think it looks like a ruby.'

'Yeah, just like the one in Mum's ring.' Luke's voice sounded excited again. 'I bet this is the snake that is the keeper of the secret treasure. He just has to be. We must be so close!'

'Let's just keep calm.' I reached for Luke and tried to hold him. I felt his chest lean heavier into my hands. I sensed danger if we crept too close. Luke tried to sidestep me. The snake jerked and spat at him, but he jumped back again, just in time.

'Stupid snake!' screamed Luke as he scuffed some gravel at it.

'Not a good idea Luke, you're only making the snake angrier.' Clare shuffled a few steps back again.

'I thought snakes were supposed to respond to vibrations? Aren't they meant to move away if they feel movement or something?' Luke stomped his feet hard on the ground, but the snake still didn't react. It continued to hold its ground.

I shone my torch around the cave for a moment to take a bit of time to think, then shone it into the snake's eyes. To my surprise, the snake backed off. I lowered the torch then raised the light to its eyes again. Sure enough, it backed away.

'That's it! It doesn't like the light. That must be why the old Balinese man had a torch.' To my surprise, Clare turned on her torch and shone the light towards the snake too.

'Yes, it makes sense, if it doesn't like light, it would hide here during the day and move out to guard Tanah Lot at night.' I agreed. With so much light shining in its face, the snake gave up, turned away and slithered towards the back of the cave.

'Keep watching it, maybe it will give us a clue on how to get in,' said Luke, forever hopeful. As we watched, the snake disappeared somewhere into the darkness between rocks and shadows. 'Did you see where it went?' Luke bent down and tried to peer through the tiny hole. 'See, there must be a secret tunnel behind here,' he continued. 'All we have to do is figure out how to get in there.'

CHAPTER 9

Secrets Hidden Below the Cave

I scanned the cave searching for another idea. The gap between the ledge the snake had been on and the roof looked to be a pretty tight fit. I couldn't see any other option, one of us would have to give it a try.

'Luke, you're the smallest, how about you see if you can squeeze up onto the snake's ledge? Maybe there's another way in from up there.'

'It's worth a try.' Luke nodded. Full of bravado and armed with a torch should the snake return, he climbed onto the rock platform where we had sat and listened to the old man's story. I gave him a little nudge from behind, and he heaved himself up onto the ledge above. First his head and chest, then he edged the rest of his body carefully forward until he could bring his legs up too.

'Can you see or feel anything?' Now my stomach was getting butterflies, this had to be the way in. I noticed Clare was on her toes, she stretched to see too, her fingers were also crossed. I guessed she was thinking much the same thing.

'There's a pile of small broken rocks right at the back.' We both strained to hear Luke. 'I can hardly reach them.'

'Stretch as far as you can,' I urged. 'Try and squeeze in a bit further.' Slowly at first, we saw one rock pushed aside, then another and another, until they were all scattered at our feet.

'I think I found a hole.' Luke's excited voice announced. There was silence for a few seconds. We heard a few faint grunts and groans. 'Yes!' Luke cried out. 'We're in!'

'Where's he gone?' Clare jumped to try to see.

'Wow! You should see this!' came a voice from somewhere on the other side of the wall.

Clare waited no longer. She scrambled

onto the ledge and hurried to squeeze through.

'Come on Zac!' I heard Luke call. 'Take in a deep breath and try to squeeze through too. I know you can do it.' Commando style, arm over arm I heaved forward until eventually the three of us stood together amazed at what we saw.

Luke was shining his torch down a long narrow tunnel of rock and tangled tree roots. The tunnel was just high enough for me to stand without needing to bend at all. I felt the sand beneath our feet. It was thick, soft and dry.

'Look!' Luke pointed to the sand with his torch. 'The snake has left a trail.' A thin winding track lead on ahead of us.

'Follow that snake's trail,' I pointed as we eagerly headed off into the unknown. The tunnel curved and weaved, and we seemed to go further underground. I noticed the number of tree roots thinning until they had all disappeared. I could smell dampness coming from the tunnel walls as I touched a few drops of trickling water. The air was cooling right down now. An eerie feeling swept over me, and I realised we could no longer hear the reassuring pounding of the ocean waves. Eventually, we turned a sharp corner.

'Wow! What a cave!'

'Cool!' said Luke.

'Awesome!' said Clare.

'Look at those limestone stalagmites and stalactites. Aren't they fantastic!'

'Yeah, Zac! But look what else!' Clare and Luke stood frozen, they stared in amazement. There in the middle of the cave was a shaft of light that unbelievably pointed down onto an old treasure chest, thick with dust, sand and cobwebs.

'Oh no! Not the snake again!' Clare took a deep breath and bit her bottom lip. 'I hate snakes!' Sure enough, it was curled up right on top of the chest. It kept its head out of the light, reared up, hissed and dared us to come closer.

CHAPTER 10

The Treasure Chest

'Stand back guys, I'll take care of him.' I tried to sound heroic. There was no way that this snake was going to stop us now. I reached for my torch and shone it directly into the snake's eyes. Clare and Luke followed my lead. I held my breath and waited. The snake gave one last annoyed hiss before it turned from the light and slithered away.

'Yes!' said Luke as he did a little triumphant dance. 'We did it!' We rushed over to the treasure chest and began to blow away the dust and cobwebs with eager anticipation. Luke rushed to brush off the rest of the sand with his hands, then, glanced at Clare then me. He began to lift the heavy creaking lid.

'Cool! There's some gold coins inside.' Luke reached in and grabbed them.

'You call them doubloons, they're old Spanish currency. Geez! Don't you know anything?' I tried to look too. I reached in and pulled out an old compass and a sextant.

'What's that thing?' asked Clare peering over my shoulder.

'It's what pirates and sailors used to use to help them navigate the seas at night. They used these to guide themselves by the stars.' I was amazed that it hadn't rusted. The gold still glistened in the light.

'There's something else in here guys!' Luke reached further into the chest.

'What is it?' Clare and I leaned over to peer further in.

'I'm not sure,' he replied as he unravelled an aged yellow cloth. Inside was written another clue, but this message was in Indonesian.

'You mean there's more to this adventure?' Clare's cautious excitement grew.

'Yes,' I replied, 'looks like this treasure hunt isn't over yet!'

Luke shone his torch around the cave. The light reflected on something silver that jutted out of the sand.

'What's that?' Luke pointed. Clare stepped over for a closer look.

'It's a pirate's sword!' Clare gasped as she started to dig away at the sand. When she went to lift it, there was a sudden movement that made her jump.

'Look! It's still got a skeleton's hand holding it.' I grabbed Clare as she jumped back and pulled her a little further away. We both stared at it for a moment. I could feel beads of sweat forming on the palms of my hands. I wanted to brush away more sand, but I wasn't sure if it was such a good idea.

Step by step, I held my breath, and I crept forward. I knelt and wiped away a bit more of the sand. The remains of a full skeleton began to take shape. First the arms, then chest, hips, legs and eventually the skull. But the skeleton was wedged under the treasure chest.

'Quick guys, help me lift the chest so I can get to the rest of the skeleton.' Frustrated,

I looked around for Luke. He was still preoccupied with the sword. He stood to one side of the cave. As he polished it, he revealed precious red, green and blue jewels. Rubies, emeralds and sapphires shone in its handle.

'Wow! This is fantastic!' He waved it around and pretended to be a pirate fighting for secret treasure.

I laughed, Luke was off daydreaming about adventures again. I continued to unearth the skeleton. My dream of being an archaeologist had come true. As I examined the skull, a gold tooth sparkled in my torchlight. I put the skull aside for a moment, eager to unearth the rest of the remains. When I reached the other hand, it became clear it too had a tight grasp on something.

A pistol, with intricate woodcarvings on the handle. I pried the pistol out of the bony hand, held it up and pointed it towards the skull.

'Careful Zac, there might still be a bullet loaded in that.' Clare sounded a bit worried. Here she went again. Such a worrywart!

'It won't still go off after all this time,' I laughed, but I couldn't resist. I had to pull the trigger, just once. I took aim at the skull, pulled back the flintlock, and gently squeezed the trigger, ...FLASH! ...BANG!

To our shock, the gun fired. The force of the blast pushed me backwards, I fell as the gun flew out of my hand. The skull exploded before our eyes. We covered our heads as we were showered with bits of bone and sand. A few stalactites fell, narrowly missing us as the bullet ricocheted off the back wall. A smell of smoke and gunpowder filled the air.

'Good one Zac!' coughed Luke as the dust settled and he brushed himself down. 'You would have been angry at me if I had done something that stupid.'

'Sshh... What was that?' Clare hugged my arm. We stood still and listened for a moment. A muffled cough came from somewhere in the darkness. Clare's voice trembled as she spoke. 'Someone else is down here.'

'Impossible.' I tried to reassure her. 'That hole was so tight it was hard enough for me to fit through. Besides, who would try to follow us?'

I peered around for a distraction. I didn't want Luke and Clare to know that I was nervous too. I looked down at the gold tooth that lay beside the crumbled mess.

'Well, at least we don't need a dentist to extract this tooth.' I laughed as I reached down to pick it up.

'That's not the only thing we'd better pick up.' Clare started to collect the bits and pieces off the cave floor as we heard another muffled cough. 'I think we'd better get out of here, Zac.'

'Yeah, you're right.' Eager to leave we started to gather all the treasures and placed each item back in the chest. I lifted one side, Clare and Luke lifted the other.

'Hang on,' I said as I thought out loud. 'We need to find another way out, we can't take this treasure chest back the same way we came, it won't fit.'

'Oh, I hadn't thought about that.' Luke nodded in agreement.

'Yeah, and I think the coughing sound came from that direction too,' agreed Clare, a frown grew across her forehead. She bit yet another fingernail. She wasn't going to have any left at this rate.

Then Luke pointed across to the tunnel on the far side of the cave. 'Why don't we try heading up there?'

'I don't know about that, Luke.' Clare bit her bottom lip. 'We don't know where it leads. We could get lost.'

'Well, we have only two choices, back the way we came, past whoever is there, or on through the new tunnel. I know my choice.' Luke continued with a determined grin. 'I want this treasure, we've worked hard enough for it, and we can't go back that way, so let's go!'

Clare moaned and picked up her end of the treasure chest.

We agreed to head into the unknown tunnel. We had no other option. About halfway along Luke dropped his end of the treasure chest.

'What is it?' Clare asked, forced to put her end down too.

'I've found another skeleton here against the wall.' He dropped to his knees to look at it. 'Cool! Wonder if he's got a sword too,'

'Have you forgotten we are in a hurry? There is someone else down here after us!' Clare glanced over her shoulder.

'Look at this,' Luke totally ignored Clare.' Wow! It looks like a gun with a trumpet on the end of it.'

'Don't point that at me guys, that's a blunderbuss!' I protested with my hands in front of my chest.

'What the heck is a blunderbuss?' Clare asked.

'It's like an old-fashioned shotgun.' I looked back at Luke, 'No! Don't pull the trigger!'

'I was just joking Zac, I'm not that stupid.'

'Put it in the chest with the other things, we can take it with us.'

'Right, let's go,' Luke picked up his end of the chest again so we could march on. His torchlight shone ahead of him to point the way.

'Wow, there's daylight up ahead already.' I picked up the pace.

'Where are we?' Clare asked as we stopped to look around. Instead of leading us deeper underground, the tunnel had led us up to an opening in the roof of a cave underneath Tanah Lot temple.

'Well that's great, how are we supposed to get down from here?' said Clare. I peered through the hole, but I couldn't see any way of climbing down.

'We're going to have to jump,' I said.

'No way!' Clare shook her head and looked around.

'It'll be okay. Just ease down as far as you can, then let yourself drop. The water will help break the fall, it doesn't look that deep anyway.'

'But there's no way of gauging just how deep the water is.' Clare shook her head.

'I'll go first. It'll be fine. The water around the temple is always shallow.' I tried to reassure her.

'What about the treasure chest?' said Luke. 'How do you think we're going to get that down?'

'Just help Clare slide it over the edge, then we'll let it drop into the water.' I answered. 'After I've jumped down, you drop the chest down. When I move it out of the way, I'll catch both of you.'

Once we were all down, we picked up the chest and started wading through the knee-deep water. We clambered over rocks, ducked and weaved around the jagged edges of the stalactites and stalagmites, and out through the cave's entrance.

We splashed through the shallow shoreline and raced as best we could with a treasure chest in tow along the sand searching for our parents. I looked around. No one else seemed to be around, or so I hoped. Most of the crowds had gathered up the top to take photos of the sunset. Had that stranger followed us? Had he kept an eye on everything we did? Was he still here?

CHAPTER 11
Cracked Codes

Luck was on our side. Mum and Dad were looking in more stalls as they too made their way up with their camera to take the iconic sunset shot. That gave us the chance to carry the treasure chest up to the car without them noticing.

'I'll go ask Dad for the keys. I'll tell him we want the towels to dry ourselves off.' I turned away from Clare and Luke. 'You two go on ahead of me. I'll meet you up there.'

We opened the back of the four-wheel drive and hid the chest under all the towels, beach bags and hats. I hoped it wouldn't be too obvious we were hiding something.

While we sat there, I pulled the old yellow cloth we had found with its message written in Indonesian from my pocket.

'Anda, something, ini, anda pertama ada something.' I ran my finger under each word. I could work out what some of the words meant. 'You, something, this, you first have something.' This was not going to be easy. 'Clare, will you look in the bags for the Indonesian translation book?'

'Sorry, Zac. We must have left it back in our hotel room,' Clare shrugged after she rummaged through everything. 'We'll have to wait until after dinner.'

'Can't we google the translations?' said Luke.

'We could if we had internet connection here, but Mum wouldn't let me have international roaming on my mobile phone. She said it would cost too much.'

'So, that means, either way, it looks like we wait till we're back at Kuta.' Clare replied.

'I guess so.' I shrugged.

The drive back and dinner seemed to take forever, but before long, we were back in our room under the blanket again. This time we had the map, the torches, the message on the yellow cloth and an English-Indonesian dictionary.

I've never seen my brother and sister so interested in a dictionary before. We flicked through the pages at great speed. It took some time, but finally, we had cracked the secret message.

YOU FIND THIS YOU MUST FIRST
HAVE FOUND MAP.
CAREFUL, WATCH OUT FOR HIDDEN
TRAP.
YOU STILL SEEK PIRATE TREASURE,
YOU HAVE LONG WAY TO MEASURE.
SMOKING MOUNTAIN YOU CAN SEE,
TAKE HOT BATH TO SET YOU FREE.

We sat staring at it for ages. Eventually, I broke the silence.

'Smoking mountain, is obviously a volcano, but which one? Bali has heaps of volcanoes.'

'What about a hot bath? What does that mean?' Asked Clare. She scratched her head. 'Not sure I like the idea of a hot bath in a smoking mountain.'

'To take a bath, you need water. So, we must need a volcano near water,' said Luke, who sounded surprisingly logical for once. 'Hot water,' he added.

'Hot spring water.' I shouted and pointed to our map spread out across my bed. 'Look! Mt Batur is a volcano with a large crater full of water, and there is a hot spring at the far end.'

'That has got to be it,' agreed Luke. 'Mt Batur, tomorrow, here we come.'

'Good luck with that.' Clare bit at the skin around a nail. She must have run out of fingernails.

'What's the matter now?' Luke grumbled.

'Dad of course. He'll want to go for a surf again if the surf's up and this is Bali. The surf is always up.'

'Then we'll just have to talk him into a tour of the volcano instead.' I said. 'I need to collect some pumice to add to my rock collection anyway.'

I don't know why, but at that moment I felt the sudden urge to look again at the treasure chest. This time, instead of looking at the things inside, I ran my hands all over the intricate wood carvings on the outside. I turned the chest over and believe it or not, there was something painted on the bottom. Puzzled, I read it out loud to Clare and Luke.

'What you see is not all real,

You must depend on what you feel.'

I looked at the blank expressions on Clare and Luke's faces.

'What on earth have I found now?'

'Maybe the gold doubloons aren't real after all.' Luke frowned.

'Maybe the whole thing was some elaborate joke, and we fell for it. Typical.' said Clare.

I could tell from the look on their faces that they were just as disappointed as me. We sunk onto the floor in silence.

'It might not be anything to do with the coins,' I said with one last attempt at hope. 'Perhaps it has something to do with the treasure chest itself. After all, that is what it's written on.' Deep in thought and rather curious, I started to run my fingers over every part of the chest. I searched for an unknown clue. We must have missed something.

'Hey guys, I thought you said you took everything out?' I could hear something slide around inside when I moved it.

'We did.' Luke assured me as he came over for a closer look too. 'What have you found?'

'I don't know yet.' I peered inside again. Sure, enough there was nothing there. I tried to give it another shake. I was certain I heard something. I reached in with my left hand, and as I placed it flat on the bottom, I measured it against the level of my other hand on the outside.

'I think I've just discovered a false bottom,' I said in disbelief. I gazed at Clare and Luke and showed them where my two hands were. They reached in with their hands too and began to feel around.

'Stop!' I demanded. 'I think I can feel a crack.' I leant in and blew away the dust. A vague outline of a narrow opening appeared.

'Quick, one of you grab my Swiss army knife out of my science kit.'

Luke rushed to my bag, found the knife and handed it to me in a split second.

'Thanks.' I slipped it into the thin crack and pried open a small panel revealing a hidden space under the false floor.

CHAPTER 12

Secrets Hidden Below the Treasure Chest

'What is it? What's in there?' Clare and Luke asked straining to see over my shoulder.

'It's a, a, … I don't know?' I reached in and pulled out a hand carved and painted piece of wood.

'Wow, looks like half a sun with a painted face.' Luke shoved me aside for a better look himself. 'But It's broken, it's been split down the middle.' He reached into the secret compartment and searched around. 'Where's the other half?' He looked like he was feeling for a prize in a lucky dip. 'It's not here,' he continued, 'the other half is missing!'

I blew the dust off the broken carving and turned it over.

'Hey, I think it's another map,' Luke's face beamed. This adventure gets better and better every day.'

'You're right,' I said. 'It looks like it could be a map of the inside of a volcano.'

'Yeah, sure guys, I suppose this will lead us to another treasure chest at the end of it too.' Clare groaned and rolled her eyes. 'A tunnel in the caves under Tanah Lot was one thing, but there is no way I am going into a volcano.' Clare crossed her arms and shook her head. 'Sounds way too dangerous to me.'

'Don't be such a wimp Clare. It's all worked out so far, hasn't it?' I stared at the map on the back of the carving. 'Besides, I always wanted the chance to explore a volcano. The question is, which volcano should we explore?'

'The other clue we found inside the treasure chest suggests we head up to Mt Batur. Maybe all the answers are up there somewhere.' Luke said as he punched his pillow and settled into his bed for the night.

'Keep dreaming, Luke,' Clare shrugged.

'Things are never that simple.'

'We'll see,' was all Luke said as he buried his head in his pillow and went off to sleep.

'I have a bad feeling about this.' Clare shook her head and nibbled at her fingers.

'Where's your sense of adventure Clare? We're seeing a bit more of Bali instead of just the beach. We're having fun, aren't we?' I paused and pointed to the treasure chest. 'You have to admit, it's been pretty good so far.'

'The snake wasn't so good.' Clare reminded me. 'Or the pistol blasting the skull to bits. That was dangerous. And not forgetting that there was someone down in the tunnel following us.'

Did she have to mention that? I didn't want to think about the fact that we were being followed. That little fact wasn't going to help me get to sleep.

Early the next morning we were much too excited to bother about eating our buffet breakfast. Well, Luke and I were excited, Clare still looked a bit nervous. I just wanted to get on the road before Dad said the surf was up again, but as usual, Dad was holding things up. He still wanted his sausages, bacon, eggs, French toast, fried rice, orange juice, coffee, cereal, fruit, the list seemed to go on forever. Just because the hotel has an all-you-can-eat breakfast, doesn't mean you have to eat everything. Dad was determined to eat as much as possible since it was included in the price of the accommodation. I looked around and noticed a lot of other dads doing exactly the same thing. Their plates were all piled high with food. Mum always said to fill up, as then we wouldn't need much lunch. I think the other parents all had the same idea.

A waiter came over to our table to clear the plates.

'Would you like more coffee sir?' he asked Dad. I looked up. It was the guy from Holland on a working holiday that had delivered us the room service that wasn't ours. 'If you would like a guide for the day,' he paused, 'or any information about certain sites, perhaps I could help you.'

'No thanks,' Dad replied. 'We've got all the maps we need and three young kids who can google anything they are eager to explore. We'll be fine, but thanks for asking.' The waiter poured Dad some more coffee. He looked like he was about to say something else but changed his mind before he walked away to serve another family.

At long last, Dad finished his breakfast. The wait had felt like forever. He wiped his face and looked at us.

'So,' he grinned. 'Surf's up.'

'C'mon Dad.' Luke groaned. 'Let's do something else today.'

Dad winked at Mum. 'I knew you kids would say that. So, what do you have in mind for today? What adventure do you have planned?'

'A trip into the mountains, to Mt Batur. You know I want to see the volcano and collect a few rocks.'

'You don't want to snorkel on that shipwreck reef? You've been nagging me about it since before we left Australia.'

'There's always time for that later. That is if you're not surfing. This would be a great day trip for the whole family.' I looked at Luke and Clare for support. Luke was nodding in agreement, Clare not quite so much.

'Looks like the volcano it is. Pack up your things, we leave in 5. Meet you beside the car.'

'How about we take a break at Ubud,' Dad suggested. 'It's a small woodcarving village about halfway to the volcano.'

'Do we have to?' sighed Luke. 'Sounds like it will be much more interesting for you and Mum than us.'

'Well I'm sure we'll all need a drink and something to eat by then anyway,' replied Dad. I grinned to myself. If Dad wasn't thinking about surfing, he was thinking about food.

I slid open the window to get a clearer look at the landscape as we drove along. The car immediately filled with the sweet smell of incense and tropical flowers. I could see the valleys were blanketed in a smoke haze, which filtered the sunlight. It reminded me a lot of the fog in Sydney on a cold winter's day, but it was hot and sticky heat here.

As we drove further north, we began our gradual ascent to Mt Batur. Once we rose above the haze, I saw the silhouette of the enormous volcano jutting through the clouds. It dominated the horizon.

'Wow! It looks just like the postcards!' I whistled. The drive continued to take us through narrow meandering roads, and passed more terraced rice fields, flanked by rows and rows of palm trees. It seemed to me that Bali was one big continuous rice paddy.

At long last, we arrived in the bustling country village of Ubud.

'Did you know Ubud is a famous art and craft centre?' Dad said as he pulled straight into a woodcarving shop. I laughed at the hens, roosters, dogs, pigs and cats that scattered in all directions as Dad tried to park the car. 'There's lots to see and explore around here.'

Mum and Dad headed straight inside to

stroll around and look at the woodcarvings on display. I stretched for a moment after being squashed in the back seat with my brother and sister and looked around the yard. There were a couple of craftsmen sitting on a verandah outside the shop, carving some sort of intricate designs. We strolled over to them for a chat. I'd rather talk to the locals than window shop any day.

'Selamat pagi. Apa Kabar, (Good morning, how are you,)' I said in my best Indonesian. The three men all laughed and smiled.

'Kabar baik,' one replied. 'So, … You think you speak good Bahasa.' The young man who spoke rose and beckoned us to come closer to the piece he was carving. 'Duduk, (sit,)' he said. 'Talk to me while I work.'

'Nama saya Zac, Clare dan Luke.' I introduced us.

'Apakah kamu orang Ingris?' Another asked.

'Tidak, dia orang Australia.' I replied.

After telling him our names, that we

were Australian, how old we were and where we were staying, he introduced himself and his fellow craftsmen.

'Nama saya Yusef, saya berumur duapuluh enam.' Yusef continued around the group with introductions, names and ages. He said he had been carving since he was a small boy of five. That meant he had already been learning the craft for twenty years. His brother, Amir, was sitting on one side of him. Amir, he told us was 30, but his grandfather who sat on the other side of him was so old, that nobody could remember his age. We all laughed, including the old man.

'We're going up to Mt Batur to look for hidden pirate treasure.' Luke announced. I nearly hit him over the head. What was he thinking? Luckily the woodcarvers didn't take him seriously, they laughed even louder.

'How do you think you will find treasure in a volcano?' Yusef raised one eyebrow. He put down the tool he was using and placed his hands in his lap.

'We have a map. It's on a carving, but the

carving is broken,'

'Sshh!' whispered Clare. She glared at Luke and poked a bony elbow into his ribs. I wished I had done that.

I wiped the sweat from the back of my neck, then gave it a bit more thought. Perhaps Luke didn't have such a bad idea after all. If they didn't take it seriously, maybe they could help. I ran back to the car and returned with the broken woodcarving. My fingers traced over the lines that we thought could be another map on the back. Then, I handed it to Yusef.

'Have you ever seen anything like this before?'

'We are looking for the other half,' Luke added.

'Since when?' Clare stared at Luke.

'Half a map isn't much good. It would help if we had the whole thing.'

Yusef glanced at it, shrugged his shoulders, and then passed it to his grandfather. He also appeared not to be particularly interested. He shook his head as he mumbled some words in Indonesian I could not understand. Disinterested, Yusef picked up his carving tool and began to work again.

The old man gently handed the woodcarving back to me. He had a strange look on his face. I sensed he knew something, but for some reason, he was reluctant to say. I had to somehow get more information from him.

I ran a hand over my head and wiped the back of my neck. What was it my Indonesian teacher said? In Indonesian culture, they show great respect for the elderly.

I tried again to hand the carving back to Yusef's grandfather, this time remembering to give it to him with my right hand only, keeping my left hand behind my back.

'Ma'af Pak. Excuse me, Please, sir,' I said as I bowed slightly. 'Please take another look. No one else here would be as wise as you.'

Yusef's grandfather smiled and turned his attention back to the carving. His old wrinkled fingers carefully traced each line of the map. He looked at it for a long time, never moving.

Beads of sweat were once again building up on the back of my neck and forehead. The heat was almost unbearable, I needed a cold drink, but I stayed put. I crossed my fingers behind my back and waited. It must have been familiar to him. Why else would he examine it for so long? I glanced at Luke. His fingers were crossed behind his back too. Clare had sat and crossed her legs. Her head rested on her hands, and she stared at the old man.

CHAPTER 13
A Forgotten Story

Mum and Dad were taking a long time to look at all the woodcarvings, but that was good. It gave us longer to talk to the old man. The expression on his face as he continued to turn the piece over in his weathered hands had me more and more excited all the time.

'You have seen this before, haven't you?' I already knew his answer. It was as plain as the nose on his face, as Dad would say.

'Ya, anak laki-laki' The old man continued so fast I had no hope understanding what he was saying.

'Whoa, slow down please Pak.' I held my hands out in front of me.

'Perhaps it would be better if I translate.' Yusef suggested with a smile. He listened to his grandfather before he began.

'Yes, my boy. I have seen one just like this, many years ago.' They both glanced around the workshop. Then beckoned us closer as they squatted on their heels and whispered.

'When I was a small boy, my cousin had one just like this. He was convinced it would lead him to a secret treasure.'

'Did he find it?' Luke asked.

'No, he did not.'

'Where does he live? Can we talk to him?'

'He lives up there.' The old man pointed towards Mt Batur.

'Fantastic! That's where we're headed next.'

'He lives in the tiny village near the lake in the middle of the volcano's crater.'

'How can we find him?'

'Everyday, in the middle of the afternoon he takes a bath in the hot spring.'

'How will we know if it's him?'

'You will know. You look. You see. You will know.'

Then the old man stood, stretched his legs, handed me the carving and walked away.

'So now what do we do?' Clare broke the silence that had fallen between us. We stood, looked at each other and watched the old man disappear into a rusty tin shed.

'We get up there and find his cousin,' said Luke. 'Maybe if we're lucky he still has the other piece.'

'Yeah, and maybe it will fit together with ours,' I was somewhat doubtful. What were the odds after all, that he would have the last piece that would fit together to complete the puzzle for our final clue?

'Come on guys!' Dad waved as he walked back towards the car. 'Thought you wanted to go see a volcano today!'

Clare jumped up from where she sat and ran to the car. That was a surprise, Clare seemed keen to be on the way. Luke and I didn't need to answer either. Mum and Dad were on their way back, parcels in hand. Mum had a massive smile on her face. She looked pleased with her purchases. Luke and I couldn't join them at the car fast enough.

As I stared out the window, I pondered on the chances of all this coming together. Luke was right, we had stumbled upon quite an adventure. I just had to keep him and Clare safe. I watched the road become steeper and narrower. Funny looking poles sprang from out the front of village houses. They looked to me like fishing rods, tall and bent with the weight of their catch. They had flowers and lanterns hanging from their tips.

'What are those weird looking things Mum?' I asked in my attempt to distract my thoughts.

'They're spirit poles, Zac.' She said. 'They are there to keep the villagers safe. The Balinese people are deeply religious in their own unique style of Hindu. They believe in spirits, ghosts and ghouls and will place flowers and food in these little temples as offerings to appease any angry deities.'

'Geez Mum, it was a simple question. I didn't ask for a lecture. You're not teaching your class now.' Mum had a terrible habit of giving you more information than you wanted. Whatever they were, I had never seen anything like them before. I had to admit they did look strange, but in a good kind of way.

At last we reached the top of the mountain. I tried to spring out of the car to get a better look at the view, but it was so hard. So many Balinese were jostling and pushing trying to sell postcards, chess sets, t-shirts, and all sorts of woodcarvings. I was frustrated. All I wanted to do was reach the lookout.

The huge crater spread below as far as my eyes could see. Rugged mountain peaks circled its rim. I could make out a few small villages and farms, scattered across its grassy sides. I smiled and watched Mt Batur's highest peak quietly smoulder in the distance. Then I saw the lake, deep within the crater. That's it! That's where we've got to go next!

I looked around for Mum and Dad, they were heading towards the restaurant.

'Lunchtime Zac!' Dad hurried up the steps. Why do grown-ups always think of their stomach first? At least that meant that over a bowl of satay chicken and nasi goreng I would be able to talk Dad into driving us down into the crater. He's always easily persuaded when he's got a full stomach.

'Can we drive down to the lake Dad?' I asked.

'Please?' Luke added.

'I should be able to gather a few good pumice samples around the lake's edge.' I ate as fast as I could and hoped Dad would too.

'We've come this far, so I don't see why not?' Dad smiled at Mum. 'Sounds like a plan.'

I felt butterflies in my stomach as we began our descent into the crater. We were so close. Would we find the old man here? Would he have the other half of the carving? I watched the road winding around the side of the mountain, through tall grass and rocky outcrops. We drove passed old crooked farmhouses, chickens, and cattle. Then, as the road flattened we found ourselves amongst what could only be described as giant black boulders. It was dried lava!

'Stop Dad! I've got to get a closer look!' I jumped out of the car and grabbed a big chunk. It crumbled like charcoal between my fingers. I found a few bits that were still hard.

'Mum, can I take some home to add to my rock collection?'

'I don't think so Zac. Look at those little bugs crawling out of some of those pieces. They're not coming in the car, and certainly not in your suitcase.' Mum frowned. 'You would never get them back through customs in Australia. One look at those creepy crawlies and the rocks would be confiscated. No Zac, leave them here.'

'Come on Zac!' Luke leant out of the car window. 'Let's get going, I want to see the hot spring. REMEMBER!'

'Okay.' I dropped the lava. I admit I was disappointed, but we did have more exciting things on our agenda. I tried not to rush back to the car. I didn't want Mum or Dad to get suspicious. They knew me too well, it wouldn't be like me to give up a chance to look at rocks that easily just because my annoying little brother urged me.

We continued to drive along the water edge and passed the burnt-out ruins of a village destroyed by a previous volcanic eruption. It reminded me of just how dangerous a volcano could be.

The hot springs appeared just ahead of us.

'Mum, can we have a swim in the hot springs while you and Dad look around?' Luke wiggled out of his clothes and grabbed his towel before Mum had a chance to answer. Just as well we already had our swimmers on under our shorts.

'Sure son,' she replied. 'Your father and I will be over there looking at some paintings and having a coffee. I'll give you half an hour, okay?'

'Thanks, Mum.' Clare and I also stripped down to our swimmers.

'Zac,' I heard Mum call back as she wandered towards the stalls. 'Don't forget you are responsible for Clare and Luke. Look out for them.'

As we ran towards the hot pool, I stopped short. Smoke was rising from the water, and the smell of Sulphur filled the air. My stomach churned. I didn't realise the smell could be this bad.

'Smells like rotten eggs.' Clare pinched her nose. 'Are you sure you want to swim in that?'

Through the haze I could see an old man, sitting in the far end of the pool. His skin was all wrinkly like a prune. He looked like someone who had been in the water for way too long. He looked more weathered and aged than anyone I had ever seen before.

'Siapa ini?' he called.

'Ma'af Pak,' I answered in the politest Indonesian I could.

'You not person from Bali,' he replied.

'My brother, sister and I are from Australia sir.'

'What your names?' He spoke in broken English.

'I'm Zac, this is Luke, and this is Clare.' But he didn't seem to look where I was pointing.

'Come, come. Join me, the water is bagus, good, bagus sekali, very good.'

We swam across the hot pool. I held my breath. There was no way I wanted to swallow a mouthful of this foul-smelling water. I could see his face more clearly once we reached him. It was pale and badly scarred. Luke and I exchanged glances. We knew this had to be the man we were looking for. His eyes were white. He was blind.

'We met your cousin in Ubud this morning. Yusef's grandfather,' I added for clarification.

'Ahh. Yes, yes.' He nodded.

'He is well and wishes to learn of your health too.'

'Ah! Saya baik baik saja,' the blind man nodded.

'What did he say?' whispered Clare.

'He's saying he's very good.' I translated, then turned back to the blind man. 'We have something to show you. Your cousin said you would be very interested.' I carefully handed him the broken woodcarving with its ornate sun face painted on one side, the carved markings on the other. His stained, burnt, and twisted fingers slowly traced over and around every part of it. A smile spread across his face.

'Where find this?' With a raised eyebrow, he sounded curious, yet concerned.

'A long way from here,' I replied. 'But do you recognise it?' I saw Clare cross her fingers, waiting for the response.

'I have one same, same. But it no good. It bring much bad luck.'

'What happened?' Luke moved closer, he appeared just as keen as me to hear his story.

'When I was boy, I hear story of secret treasure. Story handed down from father to son, many, many times.' He stopped and took a deep breath. He gasped and seemed to be in some pain. 'I think I very lucky I find carving. It show me track into volcano, I find treasure. But not true, I very unlucky. There many tunnels and caves inside volcano. I get lost. I go deep into volcano. It get hot. I smell air very thick, very bad. In tunnel I see lava.

I run, run, but volcano spirit has temper, very angry, it begin to erupt. Balls of lava fly through air. I lucky to escape. Volcano not want to let go her secret hiding place.' He then made great gestures of the mountain exploding and erupting. 'Look, my hands and face.' He exclaimed as he thrust his face and hands towards us. 'I not see a beautiful sunrise or sunset ever again.' He stopped for another breath. 'This thing no good, bring bad luck.' He rose from where he sat and went to throw the carving.

'No! Wait a minute,' I stopped him. 'You only had one half. Maybe yours and ours will fit together, then the map could be complete.'

The old blind man sank back deep into the hot water and seemed to think for a long time.

'I hide mine, many years ago. No one find it.'

'Where did you hide it?' I pleaded.

'Yes, please tell us!' Luke held his hands up in prayer.

'Please!' Clare nodded and crossed her fingers once again.

'I hide in temple, under shrine,' he finally said.

'What temple?'

'It now filled with water.'

'Where?'

'Here, the only entrance is through tunnel. Here.' He repeated, pointing at the hot spring and laughing. 'No one find,' he continued to chuckle.

Luke glanced at me, then before I could say anything, he dove beneath the water's surface. Once, twice, three times he came up for air, but he kept searching. Then, I couldn't see him anymore. Seconds turned into minutes.

'Do something Zac!' Clare shouted. 'Go after him! Where is he? Why hasn't he come back up for air?'

CHAPTER 14

Danger Looms Ahead

Just as I took a deep breath to prepare to dive to look for Luke, there was a sudden splash as he emerged and gasped for a huge lung full of air.

'You've got to see this, guys.' Luke's eyes were wide with excitement. 'You won't believe it. Follow me.' He dove again and quickly disappeared. His web of enthusiasm pulled us in. We stole a quick glance at one another, then, Clare, and I took a deep breath and dove straight in after him. I pushed off the side wall to get as much momentum as possible. We shot to the bottom of the spring and straight through a tunnel-like torpedoes racing towards a target.

Panting for breath, I wiped the water from my eyes and looked around in amazement. I heaved myself up onto a rocky ledge and sat beside Clare and Luke. The cave was littered with tiny glowworms that illuminated an incredible path to a magnificent hand-carved timber shrine.

'Wow! Unbelievable!' I couldn't believe my eyes.

'Wow,' Clare shook her head in disbelief.

'Told you so,' Luke stood and ran towards the shrine. 'Isn't it one of the most fantastic things you've ever seen?' He spread his arms out wide as he spun around. 'Just look at how intricate this carving is. The Balinese people sure put a lot of work into everything they do.' He reached up and stroked a timber monkey perched on the edge of the shrine. It had a huge grin from ear to ear. 'Do you think this monkey is hiding something?' Luke lifted the monkey to look underneath and all around it.

'Is it there? Have you found anything?' Clare joined Luke in front of the shrine.

'No, nothing so far,' Luke shrugged his shoulders. 'It has to be here somewhere, the old blind man said so.'

'Where would you hide something you never wanted anyone to find?' I stood back and scanned the cave. It was bare, except for the shrine. I scratched the side of my face. 'Maybe there is a hole in the wall of the cave somewhere.' I peered through the shadows but couldn't see anything.

'It has to be on or in the shrine,' Luke sounded hopeful as he ran his hands all over it again. Then he tried underneath.

'I think I've found it.' Luke's face beamed. 'I can definitely feel something under here.'

'Yes!' I said as I felt around too. I could feel the odd shape of the curved and broken sunrays, but it was stuck tight. 'Move your hand out of the way,' I pushed Luke aside. 'Give me a bit of wiggle room.' I crouched and held my breath. My fingers tried to wriggle it free, but it proved far more difficult than I expected.

'Luke, you grab hold too. We are going to have to pull together. Ready, 1, 2, 3, pull!'

'Yes! We did it,' Luke cried as the other half of our broken sun finally came out of its hiding place.

'Let me see.' Clare tried to snatch it from my hands. There was no way I was about to let go that easily, but I turned it around and held it up for us all to see.

'Dad's fondness of the surf and all things water sports has paid off after all.'

'What do you mean?' asked Clare.

'Do you think we could have swum down here without all those swimming lessons Dad says are essential for all Aussie kids?'

'I guess not. Growing up around water we do tend to take swimming for granted,' Clare agreed.

'Yeah, not everyone can swim as good as us.' Luke nodded.

'That's great, but now we'd better get out of here,' I insisted. 'We have been gone for a long time.'

With one last deep lung full of air we dove back into the warm water and swam back to the surface as fast as we could.

'Zac? Clare? Luke?' the old blind man asked as we regained our breath. 'You find?'

he asked reaching out a hand.

'Yes,' we replied triumphantly. 'We have it.'

'Shh!' he warned. 'Many ears can hear. Many eyes can see.' He paused for a moment, then said, 'Come, you come. We go my place.' He gestured for us to follow him.

'But there is no one else around,' I said as I looked around as far as I could see. Which, I admit, with the Sulphur heat haze was a little difficult.

'Ah, but you only think you see,' he smiled. 'Close eyes and listen.'

At first, I heard nothing but the distant banter of some village people bartering and a rooster crowing, then as I concentrated harder I heard it. A lighter clicked open and shut, open and shut. I strained my ears. That was too familiar a sound. I was beginning to feel very uncomfortable.

'I think the old man is right. I think we had better go somewhere more private.' I nodded at Luke and Clare and swam to the edge of the hot spring to get out.

'What about Mum and Dad?' Clare dried herself off with her towel and pointed towards the stalls. 'Don't you think we should tell them something?'

'Sure,' nodded Luke. 'How about we just say that we would like to explore the village a bit. Look at some of the shrines. Mum would like that.' Clare attempted a smile, but I could see she was still a bit concerned by the way she nibbled on her bottom lip. Luke in the meantime, ran over to speak to Mum and Dad briefly. He is always the more adventurous one of us, so I knew Mum would be ok with things, as long as I watched out for him.

'We have an hour,' he grinned as he returned. 'Let's not waste any time.'

The old blind man took us back to his smoke-filled timber hut. The air was thick with incense and stale tobacco. He beckoned us to sit and handed us each a bowl of boiled rice.

'Eat first,' he demanded. 'Need strength if want to face volcano.'

We sat quietly and ate until the anticipation could not be contained any longer.

'Now can we put the two pieces together? Now can we see if they fit?' I began to pace the floor, I was a bit impatient now.

'Yes Zac,' he nodded.

I raised the newly found half towards the sunlight that shone through the stained, cracked window and smoke haze. Luke lifted the other half to merge with mine. The rays from the sun disappeared from between the two halves. They were a perfect match.

'Boys, do pieces fit?' the old man whispered with a quiver in his voice.

'Yes, exactly!'

His face seemed to wrinkle even more as lines spread across his forehead.

'Hati Hati, careful. Trouble may lie ahead.'

CHAPTER 15

Secrets Hidden Below the Volcano

'Trouble?' Clare bit her bottom lip. 'What sort of trouble?'

'Bad trouble, very bad.' The old man shook his head. 'I not like you go, but be careful. Volcano, her spirit get angry quickly.'

'We'll be okay,' shrugged Luke.

'Big eagle nest up there,' he continued to warn us. 'If she lay eggs, will fight to protect babies.'

'No problem.' Luke grinned and reached inside his backpack. 'I've still got this with me!' His eyes lit up as he pulled out the blunderbuss and proudly handed it to the blind man.

'Astaga! Good heavens!' he exclaimed. 'You not have gunpowder?'

'No, of course not.' Luke reassured him. 'But I do need something to load it with, just in case.'

'Then use this boiled rice. It might help frighten eagle but will do no harm. If harm eagle, you will anger volcano spirit.' The old blind man proceeded to roll the sticky rice into small balls and ram them down the barrel with his walking stick. Luke picked up small handfuls of rice and began to help.

'We would still need a bit of gunpowder, or it won't work,' I shook my head, it was still no use.

'I have firecrackers,' the old man smiled. 'You break open, use powder.'

I wiped my mouth with the back of my hand. It seemed worth a try.

'That's a bit dangerous.' Clare shook her head.

'A little bit of powder from a cracker should be safe enough. Just need enough to fire off the rice balls.' I tried to reassure her. 'Probably won't need to use it anyway.'

'Better safe than sorry.' Luke agreed.

'I don't know.' Clare looked at the floor and shuffled her feet in the dirt. 'This is not a good idea.'

Luke ignored Clare's protests and continued to help load the blunderbuss. I studied the map in front of us that had been revealed by joining the two halves of the sun carving.

'I think I know the way,' I finally said as Luke checked the backpack for our torches and compass.

'Great!' he replied as he stood. 'Let's go!'

The old man rested a heavy hand on Luke's shoulder. He took the two carved pieces and ran his fingers over the map. 'Ah!' he said. 'Follow path that lead up eastside. When reach fork, take north path. It lead you to top of rim. Do not take first tunnel. Take second. You read map very careful then.'

'Thanks, we will. Don't worry, we'll be o.k.' Luke gave him a pat on the back before leaving.

We ran through the tiny village and on up through the grassy hills. We clambered

over huge rocks and boulders of dried lava
and on up past the many crisscrossing
bushwalking tracks. The higher and higher
we climbed, the track became steeper and
steeper. We followed the trail just as the
old man had said and took the north fork.
Eventually, we found ourselves standing,
peering over the edge of the crater. We stood
for a moment in silence and caught our breath.
Small white clouds of smoke drifted around us
as the volcano quietly smouldered, daring us
to go further.

'What are you doing?' I asked Clare, as
she scanned the sky.

'I'm looking for that eagle.' She warily
held a hand above her forehead to shelter her
face from the sun. 'No sign of it anywhere,
thank goodness.'

'So, where do we go from here Zac?'
Luke nudged and peered over my shoulder to
see the map. There were more dark tunnels
and caverns ahead than I had expected. After
careful consideration, I made my decision.
I swung down over the crater's edge and slid

onto a landing. Pushing flat against the wall, step by step, I inched towards the tunnel. Luke and Clare followed close behind.

'I can't believe I let you talk me into this.' Clare mumbled.

'It's all good,' said Luke. 'We're almost there. No going back now.'

The opening was not very high. Hunched over I shone my torch in, but could still not see very far. Together we crept in and began our descent. The tunnel turned and weaved in all directions.

The further down we went, the hotter it became. It was not long before we were wet from sweat and steam. The same smell of Sulphur from the hot spring filled the air. Still, we continued, desperate to reach the end of our treasure hunt.

It became damper underfoot. It grew slippery. I lost my footing and slid the last few meters into a small opening. Luke and Clare landed with a thump into my back.

'I need more light guys,' I tried to peer

into the darkness. Together we focused the three torches and scanned the cave. I sniffed and wiped my nose, the Sulphur smell was almost unbearable now. My stomach started to feel quite revolting. I held my breath. How embarrassing would it be if I threw up?

I had to concentrate. The walls, ceiling and floor were completely barren. Nothing could survive in here. Towards the far wall lay a simple wooden shrine. There was a stone carving, I guessed was about a meter tall, that stood in front of the shrine. It guarded whatever lay on the altar.

'What an ugly character,' whispered Clare.

'Yeah, that's enough to scare off any evil spirits.' Luke agreed as he let out a deep sigh. The shadows that fell on the gargoyle's face from our torchlight made it seem even scarier. Huddled together we crept closer. I could feel both Luke and Clare lean into me, their hands resting on my shoulders. My heart pumped heavy in my chest.

The statue had large round eyes that bulged from their sockets. The mouth gaped open, a thick, wide tongue poked out from inside. Two long sharp yellowish fang-like teeth protruded from the upper gum. Some sort of ceremonial headdress sat atop the distorted face. Dog-like ears pointed straight up as if listening for intruders. Huge wings spanned its back.

Silently, we stepped around the stone creature. Laying on the simple timber altar was a beautiful porcelain Balinese mask.

'What was that?' Clare jumped. An unexpected and sudden noise came from within the tunnel as someone slid down behind us. I heard that familiar recurring click of a lighter. My heart pounded as my torchlight shone on his rough, calloused fingers and traced its way up his overly tanned arm only to reveal the one thing I was desperately hoping I would not find. Heck! There it was, the redback spider tattoo.

'Stop!' he warned, 'don't take another step forward.'

It was the stranger from Kuta Beach. I knew it, he had been following us all along, and now he was standing, threateningly before us, with a gun pointed straight at me!

CHAPTER 16
Fight for Survival

'Don't move Emanuel!' the stranger demanded.

'That treasure is mine!' Replied a deep voice from behind me. I spun around. It was the tall Dutch waiter from our hotel at Kuta. He gave me a sly smile. He pointed a gun in our direction.

'You! Have you been following us too?'

'Yes, Zac' he said. 'I have been following you all this time. I have been searching for this treasure for years, and no upstart Australian boy is going to stop me now.'

'But there is no treasure,' Luke shook his head as he turned to point to the almost empty altar. The only thing there was the porcelain mask.

'I'm no fool boy. Now stand aside, and I'll take what's mine.'

Emanuel edged towards the front of the altar. I turned back around, the stranger with the tattoo was aiming his gun at Emanuel, the Dutch waiter, not me!

'Don't make me use this in here Emanuel,' He warned. 'I don't want to risk causing the walls to cave in with kids in here.'

'It's not fair,' cried Luke. 'Any treasure that might be there is rightfully ours.'

'Sorry kid,' Emanuel laughed greedily. 'Not a great deal you can do about it.' He waved his gun in our direction as a reminder.

'That's what you think,' Luke mumbled. Slowly he reached into his backpack as Emanuel turned towards the timber shrine. Luke slid out the blunderbuss and took aim. Just as Emanuel bent over to reach for the mask the blunderbuss fired. KABOOM!

Emanuel let out a painful yell as the blast of hard rice knocked him off balance.

'Yeah! A direct hit,' Luke punched a fist

in the air. A smell of gunpowder and burnt rice filled the air. Emanuel tripped over the statue, and his gun flew from his hand. It fell somewhere into the darkness. Rocks hit his head as they began to fall from the roof. Luke aimed the blunderbuss at Emanuel again.

'That's it! I'm outta here!' He screamed and ran back towards the tunnel holding the smouldering hole in the back of his pants. 'That bit of treasure isn't worth this much trouble.'

'Well he sure gave in easily,' Luke laughed.

'Yeah, see how fast a chicken can run,' I laughed too.

'See how funny a chicken runs with sticky rice on his backside!' added Clare as she joined in the laughter. The stranger now laughed too. He tucked his unused gun back in its holster.

Just then, the ground rumbled and shook beneath us. We all froze for a moment, in the hope it wouldn't happen again. Another tremor shook the cave, again and again, each one lasted longer than the last. Rocks began to fall all around us. The stone sculpture shook.

It became harder for us to stand.

'I think we made the volcano spirit angry after all.' Clare reached to balance herself against a wall.

'I think we had better get you kids out of here right now,' the stranger shouted above the rumbling.

'But we haven't found the treasure yet.' Luke yelled back, more determined than ever.

'Now Luke,' the man demanded. 'Forget it, it's too late.' More rocks fell, they were getting bigger. The air was thick with the heat and smell of lava and Sulphur. Tremors now continued to shake the cave.

'At least grab the mask Zac,' pleaded Luke. 'We deserve at least that.' I snatched up the mask and prepared to get out of there as fast as possible. It was difficult to run. We were tossed from side to side.

'Go!' I shouted. 'Go as fast as you can.' I tried to push my brother and sister on ahead of me. Mum would never forgive me if anything happened to them. I should have listened to Clare. We should have stayed out of the volcano.

It was not easy one-handed. The mask was a lot heavier than I had expected. The weight of it slowed me down.

'Come on Zac,' I heard Clare call. I stumbled up through the tunnel. 'Keep coming, you're nearly there.' There was desperation in her panicked voice. As I ran, I heard rocks continue to fall behind me, blocking the tunnel forever.

When I finally saw daylight, I stopped to regain my breath. I coughed several times, and the urge to vomit was overwhelming, but somehow, I held it in. I attempted to wipe some of the sweat from my face but now was not the time to stop. We were not out of danger yet. The stranger's hand reached down to grab mine.

'You're not going to take the only thing we found.' I pulled away from him.

'Don't be stupid Zac, I'm trying to help you. Give me your hand so I can pull you out of the tunnel.' The tattooed arm reached down again. I had no choice but to trust him.

We scrambled out of the crater, as the smoke grew thicker and darker. We heaved ourselves over the rim and raced down over crumbling rocks until we finally reached the grassy slopes. We slid and rolled the rest of the way down in sheer exhaustion.

'We made it.' I coughed until my lungs were clear of the Sulphur.

'Yeah,' Luke nodded. 'But we never did find the treasure.' He sat with his head rested on his knees.

'Well, at least we made it out safe and sound.' Clare stood and brushed some of the dust from her face. 'We were warned to be careful. I said this whole adventure thing was dangerous. We're still together, and no one is hurt. Isn't that what counts?'

'Sure, I suppose.' I agreed. 'Don't forget we still have the mask.' I blew off some of the dust and wiped it clean with my hand. 'You know, it is pretty neat.' I handed it to Luke to give him a little encouragement.

The mask had been ornately decorated with red sequins and gold thread on a fanned headdress of rich purple velvet. The porcelain face had been painted white, with thick ruby red lips. Black eyebrows carefully decorated in a distinctive eastern style shaped the deep-set black eyes. Emerald green and gold beads hung from the ears with soft purple balls spreading down the golden thread.

Luke stared at it for a few moments.

'These are a dime a dozen in any market stall all over Bali.' He turned it over in his hands, he was still unimpressed.

'Luke, we came out alive.' I reminded him of what Clare had said. 'That Emanuel guy could have shot us, or we could have got caught in the volcano as it rumbled and began to erupt. In fact, lava could have overflowed right down the side of the mountain, and we would be still running. I think family is all the treasure I need right now.'

I stole a glance at the tattooed stranger who was sitting regaining his breath beside me. He reached into his backpack.

'Hey.' I jumped to my feet and raised my hands.

CHAPTER 17
Final Secrets Revealed

'Chill out Zac.' The stranger laughed and pulled out a bottle of water. Took a sip, then smiled and handed it to me. 'I have no intention of hurting you or your brother and sister. I could have done that in the volcano if I had wanted to.'

'Who are you anyway?' I asked as I gladly took a sip before handing the bottle to Clare.

'My name is Hans, and I am the Curator of the Maritime History Museum in the Netherlands.'

'Then why do you have a tattoo of an Australian red-back spider on your upper arm?' I was still not convinced he was telling the truth.

'Ah,' he nodded. 'A few years ago, I

was on an expedition in Western Australia searching for artefacts for my museum, and I was bitten by one of your nasty spiders. I was so sick I had it tattooed on my arm to remind me to be more careful when I am exploring.'

'What about this Emanuel fellow?' asked Clare. 'How did he get into the cave in the volcano ahead of us?'

'He wasn't ahead of you.' Hans shook his head. 'He chased you up the mountain. In fact, he traced your every step. I followed him. That cave was so dark, and you were so concentrated on the shrine, you didn't see him skulking around you in the darkness.'

'Oh, that's creepy.' Clare shivered.

Hans then beckoned for permission to take the mask from my lap. 'May I take a closer look?' he asked. 'Yes, I guess so.' I shrugged and handed the mask to him. He examined it closely, nodded again and again, then without a word, he turned it over and let the mask smash to the ground at his feet.

'Hey. What did you do that for?' Luke yelled. 'Now we've got nothing!'

'Look again Luke.' I couldn't believe my eyes and pointed to the tiny pieces on the ground. Gold and jewels sparkled in the remaining sunlight. 'No wonder that mask felt so heavy. I was carrying the treasure after all.'

Hans bent down to pick up the jewels.

'You do realise that these belong in the Dutch museum don't you,' he said. 'However, I do believe you deserve a reward for all your adventures.'

'So, are they off a pirate ship?' Luke had to ask. His eyes beamed with delight.

'I don't think so.' Hans laughed. 'They are off a ship that belonged to the Dutch East Indies Company.'

To my surprise, he handed each of us a small handful of gold coins. 'I don't think the Dutch Government will mind too much after all this time if a little bit is not recovered.' He smiled, stood and waved us goodbye. 'See you around sometime guys, but try not to get into too much mischief, I may not be around to keep an eye on you next time.'

Hans walked over to a waiting police car. I could see they already had Emanuel in the back seat. An Indonesian Official shook Hans' hand.

'Thank you for all your support in recovering the stolen Dutch treasures. Our King and Queen will be very pleased.' I heard him say. Then Hans reached into his pocket and walked back over to us. 'Sorry,' he said, 'I should also have given you one of these.' Hans handed me one of his business cards from the Dutch Maritime Museum, he was not only the Curator but also the Chief of Archeological digs. 'Let me know if you ever want to join me on one of my expeditions,' he smiled. 'You would always be welcome.' Then he walked back to the waiting police car, sat in the front and they slowly drove away.

'What was all that about?' Mum ran towards us. 'Where have you three been? I was starting to worry.'

'You won't believe it, Mum,' Luke jumped up and down. 'We found a hidden treasure.'

'Oh, did you?' Dad winked in disbelief.

'Why don't you tell us all about it on the drive back to Kuta.'

'It all started on the beach a couple of days ago, we were digging holes and building sandcastles.' Luke's voice faded away as I half fell asleep on the back seat.

I didn't say much in the car on our way back to the hotel. Not that I had to, Luke was delighted to tell the whole story. By the time we were in our room, I had reached a decision. That evening I discussed it with Clare and Luke.

The snorkelling trip to see the reef made from the remains of the sunken WW2 Japanese ship never did eventuate. Guess there's always an excuse to come back for another holiday.

I did go surfing a few more times with Dad though, while Mum kept a watchful eye on Luke. Before leaving Bali, we agreed to use some of the gold coins from the treasure to arrange for an eye specialist to try to help the old blind man in the village at Mt Batur to see again. If it hadn't been for him, we would not have completed our journey. We left a letter and package addressed to him with the hotel reception. Our letter was brief, it simply read –

'We hope you can read this one day if your eyesight is returned and you are able to watch the sunrise over the volcano again.'

Wrapped inside the package we left the two broken halves of the sun carving, carefully glued together.

The End

Mt
Merbuk
(1388m)
Ta
Te
Ul
Te
N

Mt Batur
(1717m)
Mt Agung
(3142m)
kau
6m)
Ubud
Denpasar
ian
Sanur
Nusa
Dua

Indonesian/English Vocabulary

Bahasa Indonesia	English
Siapa nama and?	What is your name?
Nama saya	My name is ….
Siapa ini?	Who is this?
Siapa itu?	Who is that?
Apa kabar?	How are you?
Baik baik saja	Good only. (Just well)
Baik baik saja dan kamu?	Good and you?
Selamat Pagi	Good Morning
Selamat Sore	Good day
Selamat Siang	Good afternoon
Selamat Malam	Good evening
Selamat Makan	Good/happy eating
Selamat Datang	Welcome
Sampai jumpa lagi	See you later
Terima kasih	Thank you
Samma-sama	Same to you
Ma'af	Excuse me
Hari ini hari apa?	What day is it?
Hari ini	Today is…
Duduk	Sit
Hati hati	Careful
Bagus	Good (nice)
Bagus sekali	Very good
Baik	Good (well)
Selamat Ulang tahun	Happy Birthday
Selamat Tahun Baru	Happy New Year
Kepala kelapa	Coconut head
Kepala Pisang	Banana head

Days of the Week

Hari Minggu	Sunday
Hari Senin	Monday
Hari Selasa	Tuesday
Hari Rabu	Wednesday
Hari Kamis	Thursday
Hari Jumat	Friday
Hari Sabtu	Saturday

Numbers

Satu	One
Dua	Two
Tiga	Three
Empat	Four
Lima	Five
Enam	Six
Tujuh	Seven
Delapan	Eight
Sembilan	Nine
Sepuluh	Ten
Sebelas	Eleven
Duabelas	Twelve
Duapuluh	Twenty
Duapuluh satu	Twenty-one
Seratus	One hundred

OTHER BOOKS IN SERIES

The Adamson Adventures 2:
A Lighthouse in Time

When lost in a tunnel at Caves Beach on the South Coast, NSW, Zac, Clare, and Luke are rescued by a mysterious stranger. But before they get the chance to thank her, she seems to have suddenly disappeared.

Join the Adamson family on their next adventurous holiday as they follow the clues to discover a lost soul and a haunted lighthouse. Can they save the lighthouse keeper and his daughter before time runs out, or will they both be lost forever?

http://www.sandrabennettauthor.com/

The Adamson Adventures 3: Fossil Frenzy

In the drought-stricken present, the only hope is buried in the past. Devastated by the effects of drought on the family farm, Zac, has a plan. Along with his siblings, Clare and Luke, the trio head off to search for fossils. Not heading weather warnings, they must seek shelter fast when two cyclones merge to descend upon the landscape. After the storm the environment is strangely different. A lush rainforest canopy now shelters them and the homestead is nowhere in sight. Will they find the proof they need to save the farm or have they discovered much more than they ever thought possible?

About the Author

Sandra Bennett is the author of the thrilling middle-grade Adamson Adventure Series. Book One, Secrets Hidden Below, was Shortlisted in the Speech Pathology Book of the Year Awards 2019. Fossil Frenzy, book 3, was a shortlisted winner in the Queensland Writers Centre Adaptable Competition 2020, and had the opportunity to pitch the manuscript to film producers.

In previous years Sandra has independently published two picture books and two early readers. She has had eight short stories published in six anthologies.

Her story, Cyclone Kayla, was written to become a graphic novel for the non-for-profit organisation, Library For All in 2020..

As a former Primary School teacher, Sandra enjoys author school visits for talks, readings

and writing workshops. Sandra has presented
at CBCA Canberra branch and the Canberra
Writer's Festival 2019.

Understanding the importance of hooking
readers to help them develop a love of
reading from an early age, is paramount
to Sandra's passion for writing. She enjoys
creating relatable and humorous characters
in everyday situations, then turning them
into the extraordinary by giving each story a
mischievous twist.

In her spare time Sandra is often seen walking
her dog, roaming the hills around her country
property just outside of Canberra. She enjoys
creating stories that are inspired by the nature
she finds around her. Sandra's greatest and
most lovable distraction is her growing family
as more grandchildren arrive in her world.

Visit https://sandrabennettauthor.com/ to view
images from school visits and events.